The Usborne Travel Pocket Puzzle Book

Written by Alex Frith and Sam Lake

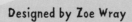

Designed by Zoe Wray

Illustrated by
Peter Allen, Mattia Cerato, Laurent Kling,
Adrien Siroy, Benedetta Giaufret and Enrica Rusinà

The Time Train has just arrived at the station...

...can you spot 15 passengers who lived in a time before trains were invented?

1 Put these pictures in the correct order to tell a story.

Find the two identical people at this funfair.

The names on the dinosaurs are all mixed up. Use the clues at the bottom to decide which name belongs to which dinosaur.

A

B

Velociraptor

Diplodocus

Clues:

Pterodactyl
(has no teeth)

Triceratops
(has three horns on its skull)

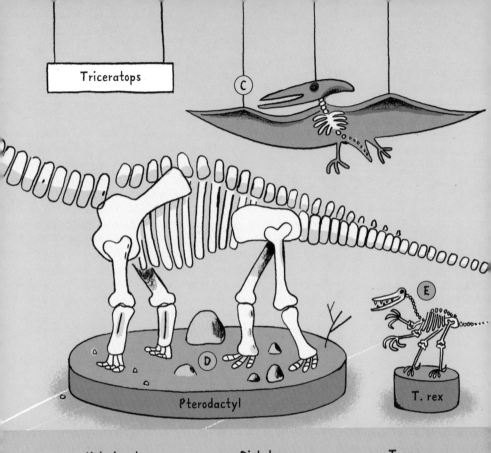

Triceratops

C

Pterodactyl

D

E

T. rex

Velociraptor
(has hands larger
than its feet)

Diplodocus
(has the
longest neck)

T. rex
(has the
largest skull)

7

Find the words hidden in the scroll.

Roman · Mummy · Ancient

Underworld · Pyramids · Mars

Papyrus · Nile · Scroll

Sword · Trojan · Myth

Warrior · Zeus · Egypt

Clue: the words can be read left to right, top to bottom, or diagonally.

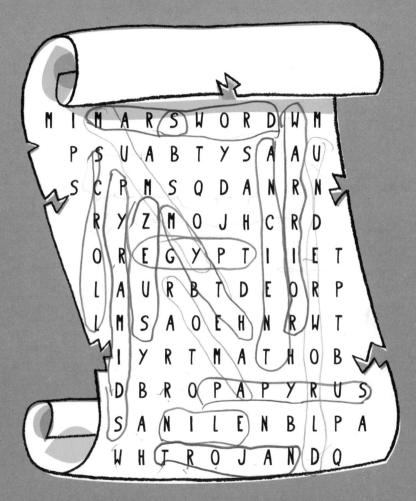

M I M A R S W O R D W M
P S U A B T Y S A A U
S C P M S Q D A N R N
R Y Z M O J H C R D
O R E G Y P T I I E T
L A U R B T D E O R P
I M S A O E H N R W T
I Y R T M A T H O B
D B R O P A P Y R U S
S A N I L E N B L P A
W H T R O J A N D Q

Which image matches the picture taken of Gill and Jen on the rollercoaster?

Match the bags in the X-ray machine to their owners.

A   4

B   3

C   2

D

1 Samson   **2** Jasper   **3** Susan   **4** Jasmine

There are 7 invisible people in the café. Can you guess where they are?

18

Find the two matching sandcastles.

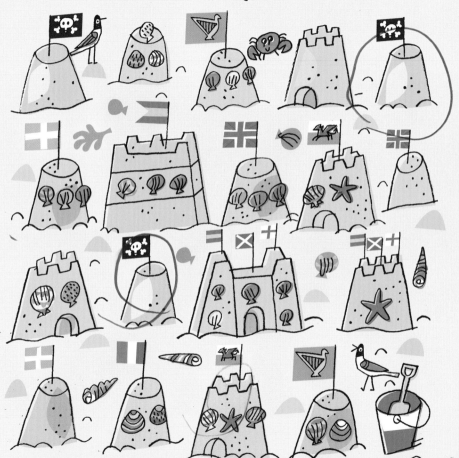

Seven objects have fallen into the aquarium that shouldn't be there!
Can you find them all?

WELCOME

Adrian

22

Adrian is looking for his friend Oliver's tent.
The only clue he has is this photograph, taken by
Oliver from the entrance to his tent.

Can you guess which tent, in the picture on the left, is Oliver's?

These visitors are looking around a new space museum...

...can you see eight differences between the two scenes?

Space suits

Meteorites

Which bus is different from the rest?

Fill in the grid with these four camping items. Each row, column, and 4-square box must contain one of each.

Tent

Backpack

Boots

Hat

Write the names in, or draw the objects.

Can you see more people on skis
or on snowboards?

The two menus on this page all say the same thing, but one uses a code alphabet.

Menu

 SANDWICH

 PIZZA

 WAFFLE

 ORANGE JUICE

 MILKSHAKE

MENU

 ΣΑΝΔ6ΙΨΗ

 ΠΙΖΖΑ

 6ΑΦΦΛΕ

 ΟΡΑΝΓΕ ΞΘΙΨΕ

 ΜΙΛΚΣΗΑΚΕ

30

Use the menus on the left to crack the code.
Then see if you can translate the menu below.

Menu of the Day

ΜΘΣΗΡΟΟΜ ΣΟΘΠ

ΣΠΑΓΗΕΤΤΙ ΒΟΛΟΓΝΕΣΕ

ΨΗΟΨΟΛΑΤΕ ΙΨΕΨΡΕΑΜ

ΦΘΔΓΕ ΨΑΚΕ

ΨΟΦΦΕΕ

32

Match the equipment below to the sports
activities on the left hand page.

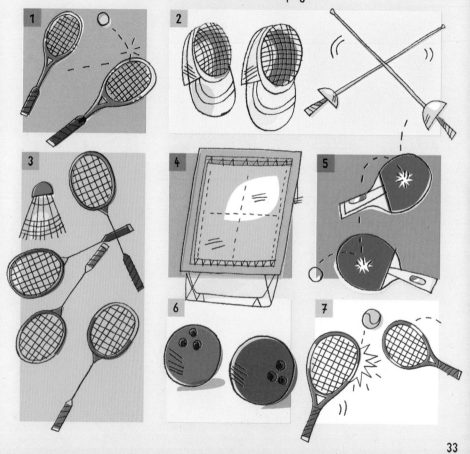

Which close-up does not match the picture on the left?

Which cactus is different from all the others?

If people using rods catch two fish each, and people using nets catch five fish each, how many fish are caught in total?

Which train goes to the seaside?

This scout troop is on an adventure camp.

Find eight differences between the two pictures.

Marcus

42

Which image can Marcus see through his camera phone?

Can you find all these things in this beach scene?

Blue flippers   A red ball   A sandcastle   Two masks and snorkels

44

A man in a rubber ring   A butterfly   A surfboard   A radio   A crab and a dog fighting   A red and blue hat

45

Log flume

Rollercoaster

Tea cups

A

B

C

Millie wants to ride on the rollercoaster.
Which line should she stand in?

46

Can you unscramble the destinations to reveal the names of five capital cities?

DEPARTURES

TIME	GATE	DESTINATION
9 0 0	4	S R P A I
9 3 0	2	T I W H G N A O N S
1 0 0 0	1	J E I B N G I
1 0 3 0	6	C W O S O M
1 1 0 0	3	I L B N E R

START HERE

48

Based on the time each picture was taken, trace the route Hans Sachertorte took to get through the swamp.

49

Can you see more motor-powered rickshaws...

...or bicycle-powered rickshaws?

If monkeys only jump onto red cars, and each car only has space
for two monkeys, how many monkeys will jump?

Move the cars so that each empty space is filled.
The letters on the cars that move will spell out two words.

Trucks must move
forward, if they can.

Red cars can only
change lanes.

Blue cars are broken
and can't move at all.

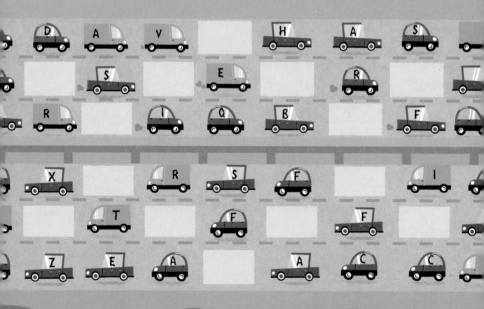

Welcome to
Las Vegas – they've
got everything here!

Can you see:

 A gigantic
guitar

 The Eiffel
Tower

 The Statue
of Liberty

 A hot-air
balloon

 The Great
Pyramid

 A rollercoaster

54

Who has the fastest slide? Add up the minutes to find out how long each loop lasts.

3 minutes

Jamie

1 minute

1 minute

Amy

2 minutes

2 minutes

2 minutes

Lisa

1 minute

1 minute

3 minutes

2 minutes

2 minutes

56

How many whole forts can you build from the parts below?
Each fort needs a tall tower, two short towers and a flag.

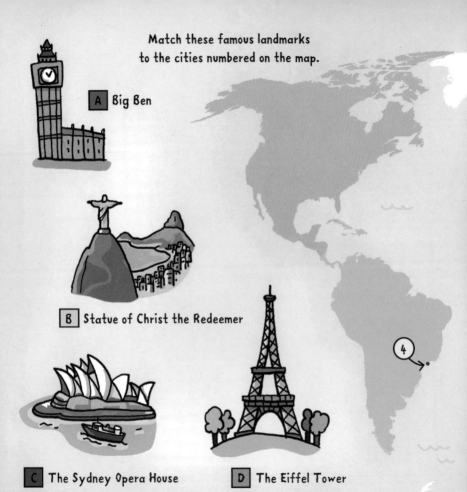

Match these famous landmarks
to the cities numbered on the map.

A Big Ben

B Statue of Christ the Redeemer

C The Sydney Opera House

D The Eiffel Tower

4

58

E The Sphinx

Can you find eight differences between this art gallery...

School

START

How can Carlos cycle home without having to pass any obstacles?

Home

63

Can you find all these items hidden in the suitcase?

Trunks	Pajamas	T-shirt
Camera	Towel	Book
Passport	Goggles	Shorts
Headphones	Sunscreen	Hat

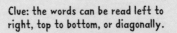

Clue: the words can be read left to right, top to bottom, or diagonally.

Match the overhead plans on top to the castles below.

Find the matching pair of inflatables.

Train

Fill in the grid with these four vehicles. Each row, column, and 4-square box must contain one of each.

Plane

Boat

Write the names in, or draw the vehicles.

Car

Van Gogh

Constable

Holbein

Francesca

Velazquez

Leonardo

Hokusai

Van Eyck

Can you find all the artists featured on the left hidden in the pyramid below?

Can you spot five people dressed as Ancient Greeks at this temple ruin?

Which statue of a Chinese warrior is different from all the others?

Which way should Alfie climb up to reach Ava's treehouse?

76

grrr

EXIT

 A The Colosseum, Rome, Italy.

 B St. Pauls Cathedral, London, UK.

In which order were these famous landmarks built?

D Stonehenge, Wiltshire, UK.

 C The Statue of Liberty, New York, USA.

 E Petronas Towers, Kuala Lumpur, Malaysia.

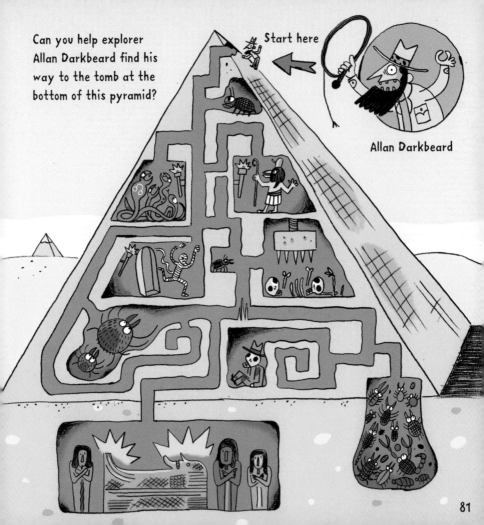

Can you help explorer Allan Darkbeard find his way to the tomb at the bottom of this pyramid?

Start here

Allan Darkbeard

81

Can you find eight differences between this Tokyo crossing...

...and this one?

Jim likes the style of these sunglasses but would prefer them in red.
Can you find the red pair?

How should the calypso drummer hold her sticks for the next step?

Is it...

A   B   C   D

The guide is leading a camel trek to Casablanca,
but whose reins is he holding?

Which food stall will please all the children?

| Fish 'n' chips | Hot dogs | Donuts | Burgers | Ice cream |

I don't like sweet things.

I love round food!

I hate fish.

I want something hot.

Which sandcastle comes next in the sequence?

Is it...

A   B   C   D

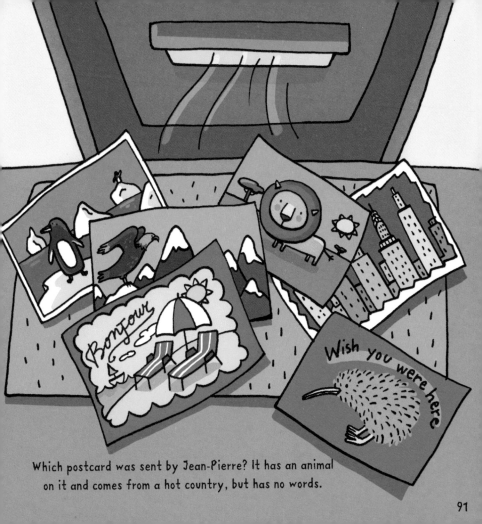

Which postcard was sent by Jean-Pierre? It has an animal
on it and comes from a hot country, but has no words.

Which of these segments doesn't come from the statue of Buddha, shown on the left?

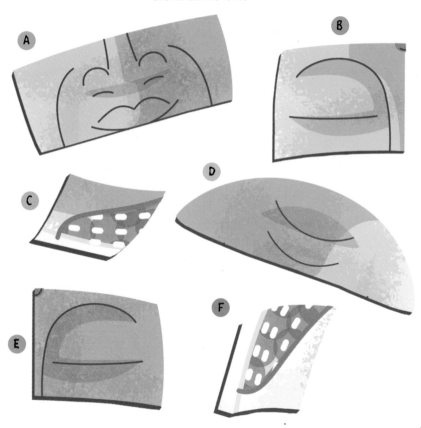

Jojo wants to visit the zoo, the castle and the mall.
Which bus should he take to see all three?

Jojo

Bus guide:

56: Mall Plaza - Museum St - Park Lane - Zoo Ave

28: Museum St - Castle Gardens - Zoo Ave - Park Lane - Pool Boulevard

119: Church Lane - Mall Plaza - Castle Gardens

254: Castle Gardens - Pool Boulevard - Zoo Ave - Mall Plaza - Park Lane

Are there more starfish or shrimp in this rockpool?

Fill in the grid with these four safari animals. Each row, column, and 4-square box must contain one of each.

Lion

Zebra

Elephant

Giraffe

You can write the names in, or draw pictures of each animal.

Can you see more frogs or lily pads in this pond?

Help the whale watchers to
find all these things:

1 lighthouse

6 sharks

4 spouting whales

2 puffins

2 dolphins

8 seals

If the distance between every stop is the same, what's the fastest route between A and E? Passengers can change trains at any yellow stop.

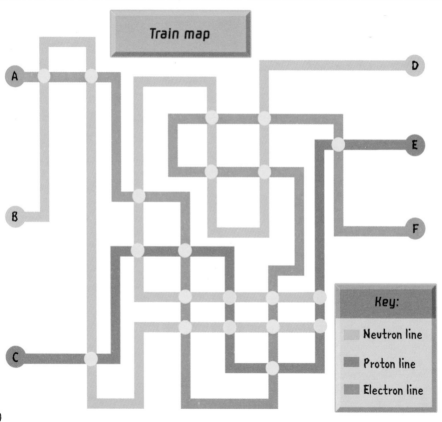

Train map

Key:
Neutron line
Proton line
Electron line

100

These Martian tourists need your help.
Use the Martian Guidebook below to translate their question.

HUMAN:

WE COME IN
PEACE. TAKE US
TO YOUR LEADER.

MARTIAN:

⊙E >▱⅂Ϝ E I∅
⅃EA>E. ⊏A⅂Ϝ U▽
⊏▱ Ξ▱U▽ ΔEAⱯE▽.

Follow these instructions to reach Camp Arawak.

Go east if you reach a square with a campfire.

Go north if you reach a square with a rockslide.

Go west if you reach a square with a bat.

Go south if you reach a square with a waterfall.

105

Find these words
hidden in the sail.

Canoe   Flippers

Paddle   Diver

Yacht   Snorkel

Waves   Surf

Kayak

Wind

W
B C I
S U E N
I S O H K D
Y N D P A P I
A A O I T Y A W
F C C R V V A D R A
R I H K E M K D H O V
W U D T E R W A L E S U E
B T S S F L I P P E R S P A S

Marcia's bag...
- is next to a pink bag
- has no stickers
- has two straps

Put the balloons in the correct order to spell out a message.

Can you find eight
stolen sandwiches?

111

Answers

Pages 2-3

Page 4

The correct order is: C A D B

Page 5

Pages 6-7

Here are the correct
dinosaur names:
A: T. Rex,
B: Triceratops,
C: Pterodactyl,
D: Diplodocus,
E: Velociraptor

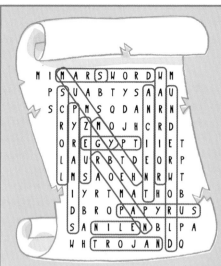

Pages 8-9

Pages 10-11
Image C is correct.

Page 12
This is the only guide book with an Indian flag on it.

Page 13

Bag A belongs to Jasmine.

Bag B belongs to Susan.

Bag C belongs to Jasper.

Bag D belongs to Samson.

Pages 14-15
Pages 16-17

114

Page 18

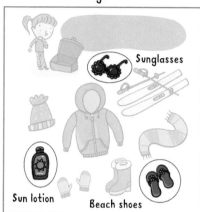

Sunglasses

Sun lotion

Beach shoes

Page 19

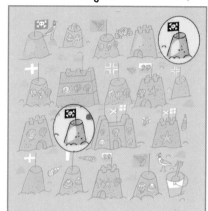

Pages 20-21

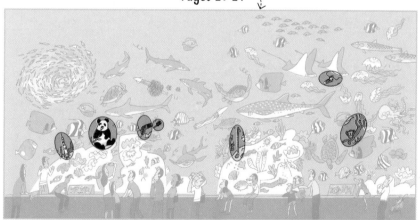

Pages 22-23

Pages 24-25

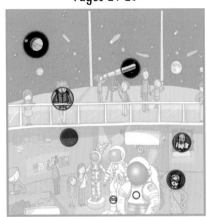

Page 26

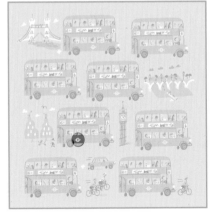

Page 27

Pages 28-29

There are 21 skiers, circled in orange, but only 15 snowboarders, circled in blue.

Pages 30-31

Mushroom soup, Spaghetti bolognese, Chocolate ice cream, Fudge cake, Coffee

Pages 32-33

A7, B6, C1, D5,
E4, F2, G3

Pages 34-35

Photo B does not match.

Page 36 ---------->

Page 37

20 fish are caught.

Pages 38-39

Train 3 goes
to the seaside.

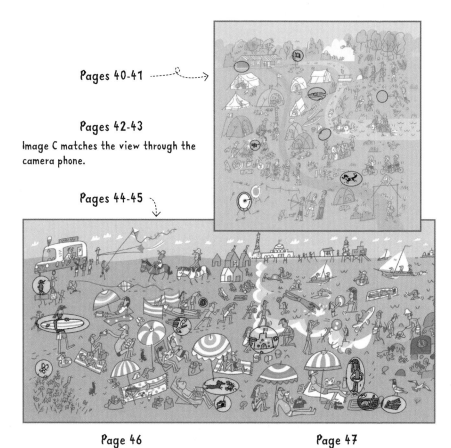

Pages 40-41 ┄┄┄┄ ⌐⌐→

Pages 42-43
Image C matches the view through the camera phone.

Pages 44-45 ⌐⌐↓

Page 46
Millie should stand in line B.

Page 47
The five capital cities are: Paris,
Washington, Beijing, Moscow, Berlin.

Pages 48-49

Pages 50-51:

There are 7 bicycle-powered rickshaws but only 6 motor-powered rickshaws.

Page 52

Six monkeys will jump.

Page 53

The hidden words are DRIVERS and TRAFFIC.

Pages 54-55

Page 56
Jamie's slide is the fastest.

Page 57
You can build four complete forts.

Pages 58-59
A1 (London, UK), B4 (Rio de Janeiro, Brazil), C5 (Sydney, Australia), D2 (Paris, France), E3 (Giza, Egypt)

Pages 60-61

Pages 62-63

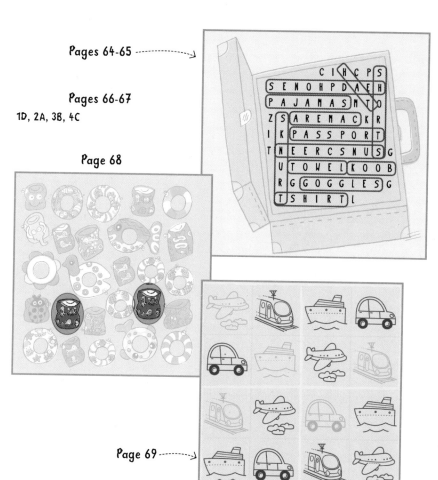

Pages 64-65

Pages 66-67
1D, 2A, 3B, 4C

Page 68

Page 69

121

Pages 70-71

Pages 72-73

Page 74

Page 75

Pages 76-77 ↑

Only route E is safe.

Pages 78-79

The blue water supply controls the red sprinkler.

Page 80

The correct order is:
Stonehenge (around 2600 BC),
The Colosseum (80 AD),
St. Paul's Cathedral (1710),
The Statue of Liberty (1886),
Petronas Towers (1998).

Page 81 ----->

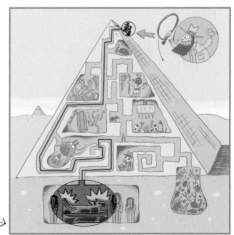

Pages 82-83

Page 84

Page 85
Position A is the next in sequence.

Pages 86-87

Page 88
The guide is leading Ilsa.

Page 89
Only burgers will please everyone.

Page 90
Castle B is next.

Page 91 ---->

Pages 92-93
Segment D does not match the statue.

Page 94
Only bus 254 stops at all the places Jojo wants to see.

Page 95
There are 12 starfish but only 9 shrimp.

^--- Page 96

Page 97
There are 14 lily pads but only 10 frogs.

Pages 98-99

Pages 101

The aliens are saying, "Will you take our picture?"

Pages 100

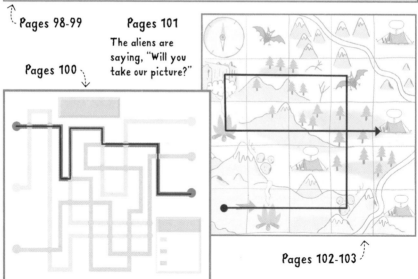

Pages 102-103

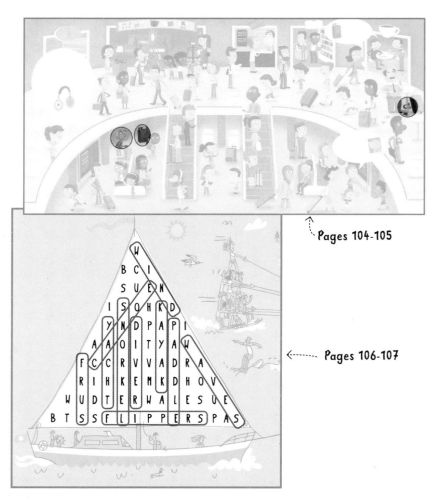

Pages 104-105

Pages 106-107

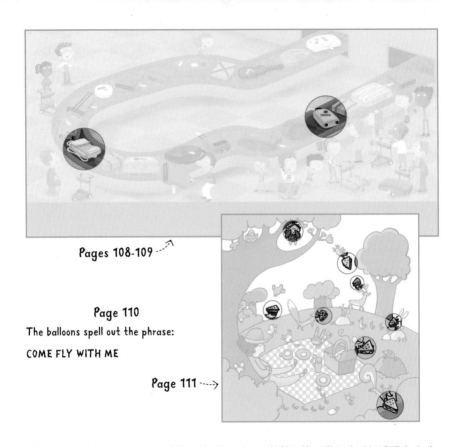

Pages 108-109 ---↗

Page 110

The balloons spell out the phrase:

COME FLY WITH ME

Page 111 --->